GW01237455

24 HOUR RENEWAL HOTLINE 0845 607 6119
www.cornwall.gov.uk/Library

All the people in High Town liked Jack. Jack liked to help people and he never wanted a reward in return.

Most of all, Jack liked to fix things. People often saw him walking around High Town looking for things to fix and people to help.

When Mr Brown's old radio broke, Jack fixed it.

"Thank you. I must reward you in return for fixing my radio," said Mr Brown.

"I'm happy with just a 'thank you'," replied Jack.

Jack fixed Mrs Curl's bike when it broke. Mrs Curl was very happy.

"Thank you! As a reward, I must make a pie for you," she cried.

"I'm happy with just a 'thank you'," replied Jack.

Mrs Crown was rolling the cricket pitch flat for a game. The roller broke and rolled off towards the pond.

"Quick! Somebody help!" shouted Mrs Crown.

"I'll get it!" shouted Jack. He ran after the roller, pulled it out of the pond and fixed it. Then he returned it to Mrs Crown.

Mrs Curl said, "Let's give Jack a reward in return for all of his help."

"He can have my dad's old car if he can fix the engine," a boy said. They all agreed.

Jack frowned. He had never fixed a car before. He didn't want a reward, but his friends had done a kind thing and he didn't want to hurt their feelings.

"Thank you. I'll try," said Jack with a sigh.

All of the people in High Town came to see if Jack had fixed the car.

He turned the key to start the engine. Nothing happened. He tried it again and …

… the engine burst loudly into life! The car lurched forwards and gave Jack a fright. He held on to the steering wheel tightly.

The car went faster and faster.

"Get out of the way!" Jack shouted. He and the car were soon out of sight.

At last, Jack found the brake. He drove around and stopped the car next to his friends.

"Thank you all, but I think I'll stick to walking!" said Jack.

car
Why did the people of High Town give Jack the car?

Jack
What did Jack say when people wanted to reward him?

radio
Whose radio did Jack fix?

High Town
Go back to page 5 and describe High Town.

fright
What other words do you know to describe how Jack felt?

roller
What was Mrs Crow doing when the roller rolled away.

Notes for Parents and Teachers

Popular Rewards Early Readers have been specially created to build young readers' vocabulary, develop their comprehension skills and boost their progress towards independent reading.

★ Make reading fun. Why not read the story and have your child clap when they hear a featured phonics sound, then race to find it on the page?

★ Encourage your child to read aloud to help pick up and resolve any difficulties. As their skills grow, it will also help their fluency and expression.

★ The list of phonics sounds and 'tough and tricky' words will to help consolidate their learning, and the questions will develop comprehension and communication skills.

★ Always keep a positive attitude and focus on your child's achievements. This will help their confidence and build their enjoyment of reading.

ISBN 978-1-78270-224-5

Illustrated by Chris Rothero

Copyright © Award Publications Limited
Popular Rewards® is a registered trademark of Award Publications Limited

Published by Award Publications Limited,
The Old Riding School, Welbeck, Worksop, S80 3LR

18 1

Printed in Estonia